Love from
Paddington

Michael Bond

Love from
Paddington

Illustrated by
Peggy Fortnum *and* R.W. Alley

HarperCollins *Children's Books*

First published in Great Britain by HarperCollins Children's Books in 2014

13 5 7 9 10 8 6 4 2

HarperCollins Children's Books is a division of HarperCollins*Publishers* Ltd,
1 London Bridge Street, London SE1 9GF.

Visit our website at:
www.harpercollins.co.uk

ISBN: 978-0-00-759418-4

Originated by Dot Gradations Ltd, UK
Printed in Great Britain by
Clays Ltd, St Ives plc

MIX
**Paper from
responsible sources**
FSC
www.fsc.org
FSC® C007454

FSC is a non-profit international organisation established to promote the
responsible management of the world's forests. Products carrying the FSC
label are independently certified to assure consumers that they come
from forests that are managed to meet the social, economic and
ecological needs of present and future generations.

Find out more about HarperCollins and the environment at
www.harpercollins.co.uk/green

CONTENTS

A LETTER FROM MICHAEL BOND

Dear Reader

In a world that has rapidly accustomed itself to communicating by email, Paddington is equally rapidly becoming something of an oddity, for he steadfastly remains wedded to what has become jocularly known as SNAIL MAIL, and long may it remain so, for there is nothing quite so heart warming as a hand-written letter.

In Paddington's case, being a bear, the use of a keyboard is too tedious for words because each stroke of a paw embraces a half dozen or so characters, which is no use to man nor beast. Short of pressing each key down with the aid of a pencil, which is too tedious for all but the shortest words, there is no way out of the problem.

Luckily, nearly all his letters are written to his Aunt Lucy, who lives in the Home for Retired Bears in Peru. Luckier still, being a wise old bear she has kept them all, for she foresaw how valuable they would become with age.

If you are new to Paddington, then you will find lots of fresh stories to read and enjoy. If you have encountered them all before, then they will still make fun reading, for they are Paddington's take on his many adventures, which are not necessarily the same as that of the other characters involved.

Either way, there is something for all who simply enjoy a good read.

Yours truly

Michael Bond

Preface

One night, many moons ago, the ocean liner *S.S. Karenia* left the Peruvian port of Lima in South America and set sail for Europe.

There was nothing unusual in that, for it was a regular crossing carrying as many passengers as it could take, along with a full crew to look after their every need during the voyage.

However, on this particular occasion, unbeknown to the Captain, they had a stowaway aboard. He had been smuggled onto the ship at the very last moment by his aunt, and he was hiding under a sheet of tarpaulin in one of the lifeboats.

"Now, promise me you will write," she said, as the liner's siren gave an impatient wail that echoed round the harbour.

"I promise to write as soon as I get the chance," said the bear.

"I've filled your suitcase with jars of marmalade for the journey," said his aunt. "And I have paid one of the crew to make sure you never run short of drinking water."

While she was talking she tied a large label round her nephew's neck. "I've knotted the string twice over," she said, "so it shouldn't come apart. But you may find it very useful, so do take care of it."

"Thank you, Aunt Lucy," said the bear, raising his hat. "You are very kind." He would have preferred cocoa, but he was much too polite to say so.

In any case there was no time for more as the gap between the *Karenia* and the quay began to widen and his aunt had to make good her escape by sliding down a rope.

She only just managed to avoid falling into the harbour and by the time she had righted herself a wall of darkness separated her from the lifeboat.

She wiped away a tear as she waved a last goodbye into the pitch black night. "I hope I've done the right thing," she said, when she arrived back at the Home. "It feels as though I have lost a part of myself."

"Of course you've done the right thing," said

the oldest inhabitant. She stopped knitting and set her rocking chair in motion to emphasise the point.

"This is no place for a young cub full of the joys of spring. That bear needs to go out into the world. We shall hear more about him before the year is out … you mark my words."

"I wish I'd given him a good book to read," said Aunt Lucy.

"You will need one yourself by the time the *Karenia* reaches the end of its journey," said another bear.

"It's always worse for the one who stays behind," she added.

And she was right, for Aunt Lucy soon lost count of the number of raffia table mats she made while she awaited news. Luckily it was the tourist

season, so they soon disappeared from the stall permanently outside their building.

Then one day a postman arrived brandishing an envelope, the front of which was festooned with blue labels and strange-looking stamps.

It was addressed to Aunt Lucy, c/o The Home

for Retired Bears, Lima.

By popular request, Aunt Lucy dropped the table mat she was working on and began reading the contents of the letter out loud to the other bears.

"Dear Aunt Lucy, I..." she began, before pausing for a moment as the next word seemed to have been crossed out for some reason.

"I eggspect expect this will come as a great surprise to you, but not only have I arrived in England, but I have an address!

"I'm staying at number 32 Windsor Gardens and it isn't at all like the Home for Retired Bears. You may not believe this, but it's very near the Portobello Road, which you have often talked about when you suggested I might like living in London.

"I have been taken in for the next day or two by a nice family called the Browns, but I'm hoping it will be much longer than that because I am very happy here. I have my own bed, so I am on my best behaviour, which isn't easy because I have already flooded their bathroom by mistake and a lot of the water went through their downstairs ceiling. The trouble is I'm used to sitting in a puddle after it rains and I had never been in a bath before.

"Luckily the drips landed on their two children, Jonathan and Judy, who came to my rescue.

"But then, as I said to Judy when I first arrived, 'Things are always happening to me. I'm that sort of bear.'

"In fact, it is Judy who is typing this letter because she noticed straight away that my spelling isn't very good. Also, using Mr Brown's computer isn't easy with paws as I can't help touching several keys at the same time. This is an example of what happens when I try to type the letter 'i' – uhiyg …!"

Aunt Lucy held up the letter for the others in the room to see.

"I find using a pencil to poke the keys is the best way to do it," she read. "But that takes much longer.

"I wrote several letters to you while I was in the lifeboat on the way over. That took even longer because I used marmalade chunks instead of a pen, so the writing wasn't very clear. I put them one by one inside the empty marmalade jars, screwing the tops on tightly before throwing them into the sea. I expect they might turn up one day, but you won't have missed much if they don't.

"All I could think of to say was, 'I hope this doesn't find you as it leaves me,' and there aren't any signposts in the middle of the ocean so, as I had no idea where I was at the time, they aren't very interesting.

"Jonathan is sending this note by something called AIR MAIL, so you will get it as soon as possible. I will write again tomorrow because I have another big surprise for you. Love from PADDINGTON."

Aunt Lucy had trouble with the last word. "I don't know what that means," she said, "but someone else has added a bit more at the end."

"Hello Aunt Lucy," she read. "And a big hello to everyone else in the Home for Retired Bears.

We have been hearing all about you. Don't
worry. We will look after him and the odd job
man is already working on the ceiling. Judy."

As she reached the end all the other bears
applauded.

The sound was not unlike the gentle lapping of the sea as it entered the harbour, for paws are not really meant for clapping.

"If only my nephew could hear it," thought Aunt Lucy. "He *would* be pleased. I must send him a postcard straight away."

Letter No. 2

Dear Aunt Lucy,

Thank you very much for your postcard showing Lima harbour with the tide coming in, which arrived yesterday. I'm sorry if my letter made you ankshush (anxious — Judy). The funny word you came across at the bottom and you didn't understand is my NEW NAME! I hope you are sitting comfortably so that I can tell you how it came about.

When I arrived in

England I had no idea where I was or which way to go, so I waited in the lifeboat until all the people on the *Karenia* had disappeared. Then I stowed away on a train marked to LONDON, which is where you hoped I would end up.

I sat very still and when the man who collects the tickets came round and saw the label you tied round my neck, he must have thought I was a parcel.

It's lucky bears are good at stowing away because when the train reached London it couldn't go any further and I found myself on a strange railway platform near the Lost Property Office.

It was very busy. Everybody else was in a hurry and they seemed to know where they were going, so I sat on my suitcase and waited for something to happen.

Which was how I met Mr and Mrs Brown.

They were there to meet their daughter, Judy, who was coming home for the school holidays, when Mr Brown spotted me. Mrs Brown didn't believe him at first, but when she saw my label and read the words '*PLEASE LOOK AFTER THIS BEAR. THANK YOU!*' she said at once I must come home with them. I think your adding the words 'thank you' must have made all the difference, because if they had left me where I was there would have been nothing to thank them for.

After all, they could have left me in the Lost Property Office, or left me where I was and gone on their way, but they didn't do either of those things.

Mr Brown asked me what my name was, but when I told them Mrs Brown had trouble saying it, so she decided to call me after the place where we met, which is how I came to have such an unusual name for a bear, because PADDINGTON is the name of the station.

I like it myself, so I hope you do too. Mr Brown says it sounds important and Judy's brother, Jonathan, told me I might have ended up with a name like CHARING CROSS or WAPPING, which are nowhere near as nice.

Another thing, Aunt Lucy, it's good that you taught me to speak English when I was small, because not many people in England speak Peruvian.

I went on an Underground train yesterday for the very first time. We were going on a shopping expedition so I asked everyone in the carriage if they spoke Peruvian and no one did. Mind you, not many of them spoke English either!

Mrs Brown bought me a dark blue duffle coat to keep out the cold and Jonathan gave me something called an INK PAD so that when I write a letter to anyone I can make a paw mark to show it is genuine. I don't suppose many bears have their very own ink pad.

I think perhaps it means I might be staying with them for more than a few days. I do hope so. Judy hopes so too. She says WATCH THIS SPACE!

love from
Paddington

Letter No. 3

Dear Aunt Lucy,

The drawing at the top of this letter is what
Jonathan told me will one day be called an

29

HISTORIC DOCUMENT if it isn't already, and I thought you might like to have a copy before I am very much older. There is another one to go with it.

The original was made by a friend of the Browns and it shows me taking a picture of the whole family group on a very old camera. It's called a 'plate camera' and I expected it to be a

dinner plate, but it's what the picture showed up on before they invented film.

It's only a back view of the Browns I'm afraid, but it will give you a good idea of what they look like.

It's a good job you can't see Mr Brown (he's the one in the middle) because I was having trouble focussing the camera and he was cross because by then they were sitting in his bed of prize petunias, but I had to get it right first time because there was only one plate left and you can't get them any more.

Well, it wasn't just that. Jonathan suggested I used a piece of string to measure the distance and I tied the far end onto Mr Brown's ear by mistake. (I thought it was one of his petunias until I pulled it tight!)

The one on the left is a lady called Mrs Bird. Judy told me she has a bun in her hair. I thought it was in case she got hungry – a bit like me keeping a marmalade sandwich under my hat in case I have an emergency – but apparently she does the cooking and she likes it tied up out of the way. I expect it stops it falling into the saucepans.

The one next to her is Judy. Then, on Mr Brown's right, there is Jonathan, and last of all, Mrs Brown.

I had to put my head under a black hood at the back of the camera in order to take the picture and all I can say is it's a good thing you don't have to take pictures on a plate any more, because as you can see in the other sketch I lost my way and nearly fell in some rose bushes.

Mr Brown said, "Can you picture what the

world would be like if everyone taking pictures with their camera had to wear a black hood?"

He was looking at me while he said it.

Anyway, there was a happy ending because when he took the camera into a photographic shop the man was so pleased he put it in his window with a notice saying it was owned by LOCAL BEAR GENTLEMAN and he promised to make some copies of the photograph, so you will get to see what they all look like when you see them the right way round.

love from
Paddington

Letter No. 4

Dear Aunt Lucy,

Judy asked me why I number my letters to you instead of dating them. I told her it's because bears don't have calendars. I hope that's right. I said if you are a bear, one day is very like another

and we go by seasons. It's either hot or it's cold. (Except in England where it never seems to be the same two days running.)

She also asked me how I keep the postcards you send

me in the right order. I explained I have an elastic band, and she said, "Everybody has their methods!"

But this is a special letter, so I think you may want to pin it up on the notice board along with the week's dinner menus, because it might turn out to be HISTORIC like the last one.

Mr Brown has made up his mind at long last. I am here to stay! Best of all, I shall be moving out of the guest room and I shall have a room all to myself at the top of the house. You could say it's like living in a tree as I did when I was small, but this time it has a wall on all four sides and a door.

Mr Brown said he is doing it up specially. All the bits and pieces arrived in a van this morning and the driver very kindly took them upstairs for us instead of leaving them in the hall.

There is a big can of whitewash, some paint,

several rolls of wallpaper with flowers on it and a big bucket for the paste, lots of different brushes and a folding table.

When I asked him what they were all for he gave me a funny look and said, "It's what's known as Do-It-Yourself, gov.," and he wished me best of luck.

I don't think he had met a bear before because he drove off very fast.

That was last week and Mr Brown, who is something in the city, has been keeping what Jonathan says is called 'a low profile' and he hasn't had a chance to touch them, so the other day when I was at a loose end and everyone else was out of the house I thought I might help him out by 'Doing-It-*Myself*' instead.

It seemed a good idea at the time and I really

don't know what went wrong, it all happened so quickly. First of all the wallpaper wouldn't stay up. Every time I tried fastening a sheet to the wall it fell off and landed on top of me. One thing led to another and by the time the others returned home I was completely covered.

Jonathan was first up and he said, "Crikey! I bet you put too much water in the paste! I've never seen such a mess." I think he was wishing he'd done it himself instead of me.

Judy took one look and said, "Awesome!"

Mrs Brown was asking everyone where something called 'smelling salts' had got to, and Mrs Bird said it ought to teach them all a lesson never to leave me alone in the house again.

I expect you are wondering who Mrs Bird is. Well, she is a distant relative of Mrs Brown. She lost her husband in a war and instead of living on her own she looks after the family.

She can seem a bit fierce at times, but I think she likes me, and she also knows all there is to know about bears. The first thing she said when she heard I might be staying for a while was,

"I had better get some more marmalade in." I expect that's because I raised my hat and she likes polite people. Most people in England don't wear a hat these days so it probably doesn't happen to her very often.

Anyway, she sent me off to have a bath before

my fur set hard and to my surprise, one way and another, instead of being cross with me, everyone seemed very pleased.

Judy said although it was awesome, I shouldn't worry because Mr Biggs, the odd job man, has promised to put things right while he's here to repair the ceiling and she was to say 'thank you' on his behalf because he needed the work and he gave me what he called 'a little something'.

Mrs Brown gave me some extra pocket money because the room was about to be done properly at long last.

Mr Brown added to it when he came home because he hadn't really wanted to do the job in the first place.

Mrs Bird said she wasn't at all surprised because bears usually fall on their feet.

I'm very well off now, so I may try doing some more decorating if I ever run short.

love from
Paddington

P. S. Thank you very much for the postcard you sent me showing a picture of Lima harbour with the tide going out. I keep it by the side of the bed in my new room alongside the picture I have of you. Yours is in a frame, of course.

Letter No. 5

Dear Aunt Lucy,

I'm sorry you haven't heard from me lately, but after my last letter Jonathan and Judy went back to school and I have been kept very busy.

Mrs Bird told me there is an old proverb which says 'Young bears ought not to be idle. It's bad for them'. So when I told her they are very good at shopping she first

of all persuaded Mr Brown to buy me a basket on wheels, then she showed me round the market in the Portobello Road.

I soon got to know all the stall keepers, and in no time at all I found myself going there every day of the week except Sundays.

That's because I have made friends with someone extra special. His name is Mr Gruber and he keeps an antique shop. The Browns are all lovely people, but Mr Gruber is especially nice. He was born in Hungary, but he spent some time in South America before coming to England as a refugee. So, as he says, "We have a lot in common".

Mrs Bird is so pleased with my shopping she says I am worth my weight in gold, which is very nice to know.

I tested myself on the bathroom scales the other day. I won't tell you how much I weigh, but I always look both ways now before I cross the road in case I get run over.

In the meantime she gives me extra pocket money, so I now have what's known as a standing order for buns in the bakers near Mr Gruber, and because we both like cocoa, he has some ready every day and we share our 'elevenses' sitting on a sofa at the back of his shop.

His shop is usually full of interesting things. You would think that being old they would be cheaper than something new, but the reverse is true; very often the older they are, the better.

They come and they go, and I sometimes wonder where they all come from in the first place. Then one day I happened to notice that it was less full than usual.

Mr Gruber looked very pleased when I told him.

"It's nice that you take such an interest in my business, Mr Brown," he said. "I had a busy day yesterday after you left. A big party of American visitors descended on me. As a matter of fact I'm going to an auction sale this very afternoon in order to stock up."

I told him we didn't have auction sales in

Darkest Peru and he thought for a moment. "It's hard to explain, Mr Brown," he said. "They are places where things are sold to the highest bidder. Why don't you come with me and see one for yourself."

Can you imagine, Aunt Lucy? I was so excited I ran all the way back to Windsor Gardens and had a bath specially so that I wouldn't let him down.

Mrs Bird thought I was sickening for something, but when I told her the reason she was excited too. "I hope Mr Gruber recognises you," she said.

He certainly did, and as we entered a big hall lots of people recognised him, even though he was wearing his best suit.

He led me through the crowd towards a big platform where there was a man shouting out things through a microphone.

He was talking so fast I couldn't understand a word he was saying, and nearby there was a man waving in our direction.

I must say I was a bit surprised Mr Gruber didn't wave back because he's always so polite, so I raised my hat for him instead.

The man who was waving looked rather cross and he waved even harder, so I raised my hat again. If I did it once, I did it a dozen times before he stopped.

At which point the man on the platform

changed his tune. "GOING," he shouted, waving
a hammer in the air. "GOING ... GOING ...
GONE!" And he hit a table with a very loud bang.
Sold to the young bear gentleman
who's just arrived."

"Oh dear," said
Mr Gruber. "I'm
afraid you have just
bought a boxful of old
carpentry tools."

I very nearly fell
over backwards with my legs in the air.

Mr Gruber looked most embarrassed. "It
was entirely my fault, Mr Brown," he said.
"I should have warned you before we came.
It's very dangerous giving any kind of signal at
an auction sale.

"If you nod your head or even scratch your nose the auctioneer takes it as a sign that you are making a bid for what is on sale."

I tell you, Aunt Lucy, I didn't blink an eyelid for the rest of the time we were there.

love from
Paddington

P. S. For some reason Mrs Bird didn't look too pleased when she heard what I had bought. "I think you had better do any carpentry in the garden," she said, and it was put in Mr Brown's shed for the time being.

Letter No. 6

Dear Aunt Lucy,

I haven't told you about the Browns' next-door neighbour before now because they don't like talking about him if they can help it, and I can see why. His name is Mr Curry and he is always wanting something for nothing.

Jonathan thinks that when he was small he must have fallen out of his cot on the wrong side one day and he's been in a bad mood ever since.

He also likes peering through knotholes in our garden fence to see what's going on.

I didn't realise it at the time but he must have

been looking through one the very next morning when I had my carpentry outfit out on the lawn and I was going through all the tools to see what they looked like.

I was testing the hammer on some concrete, pretending I was an auctioneer, when there was a shout from next door and I nearly jumped out of my skin with fright when I looked up and saw Mr Curry glaring at me over the top of the fence.

"What are you doing, BEAR?" he bellowed. "I can't hear myself think."

"Do it yourself, Mr Curry!" I said. It was the first time I have ever seen anyone's face go purple just like that.

"How dare you talk to me like that, BEAR!"
he spluttered. "I've a good mind to report you
to Mrs Bird."

That was when I made my second mistake.

"I thought you were an antique," I said.
"Mr Gruber often says old things are worth
much more."

I thought his eyes were going to pop out and
I did my best to explain that Mr Brown had given
me some plywood and a book of instructions
to go with my carpentry outfit so that I could
make him a magazine rack.

The book was called *Delight Your Family and
Surprise Your Friends* and I was about to start
work.

It seemed to do the trick. Mr Curry calmed
down and for a moment or two I thought he

was trying to wash his hands, but I couldn't see any soap.

"A magazine rack?" he repeated. "I wouldn't mind one of those, bear. If you make me a magazine rack I shan't report you to Mrs Bird."

He went on to say he would be out for the rest of the morning, but I could use his kitchen table to work on. It would be so much better than trying to do it on the lawn. "Besides," he said, "I'd rather you didn't tell the others or they will all want one. I suggest we keep it a secret between ourselves."

Unfortunately, although it seemed a good idea at the time, Mr Curry's kitchen table was much smaller than Mr Brown's sheet of plywood.

The plywood was so big it needed to be cut in half anyway, if I was going to make two magazine racks, so after I had put it on the table I climbed on top of it armed with the saw.

It went through the first bit like a knife through butter, but after that things seemed to get harder and harder. In fact, I had to stop and mop my brow several times before it suddenly got easier again.

That was when I had my second shock of the morning. I just managed to jump clear before everything collapsed around me.

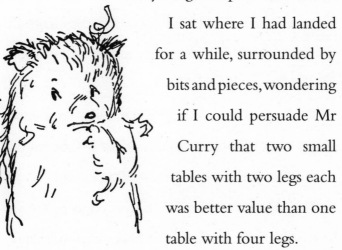

I sat where I had landed for a while, surrounded by bits and pieces, wondering if I could persuade Mr Curry that two small tables with two legs each was better value than one table with four legs.

In the end I decided it wouldn't be a good idea to make his face go purple twice in one day so, having found a tube of glue, I used up the whole lot on both the newly sawn edges of the table. Then I propped them together and put some old saucepans underneath to support it while the glue dried.

With the lights out and the curtains drawn it could have looked worse, especially after I spread some marmalade over the join as a finishing touch, so I went back to making the magazine racks and hoped for the best.

A lot more happened before the end of the story, Aunt Lucy, but I am running out of ink. However, as Mr Brown's instruction book said: My family were delighted with the magazine racks I made and Mr Curry couldn't have been more surprised.

The last I saw of him
he was running round
and round his garden
brandishing half a table
shouting, "BEAR! Where
are you, BEAR?"

It was Mrs Bird who
came to my rescue while
I hid behind the dining-
room curtains.

She told Mr
Curry it wasn't
true to say you
can't please all
the people all
the time, and
she made him

a present of my carpentry outfit, so everyone

was happy, including me!

love from
Paddington

Letter No. 7

Dear Aunt Lucy,

You will never guess what happened to me last week. Mr Gruber took me to see the Changing of the Guard at Buckingham Palace. He had his camera with him and he gave me a Union Jack flag on a stick in case I saw the Queen.

I tried waving it through the railings, but I think she might have been out doing her shopping because nobody waved back and a policeman moved me on in case I got my head stuck.

The Palace is much bigger than the Home for Retired Bears. Instead of having a caretaker like ours who's away most of the time and as you sometimes say needs changing when he *is* there, this one is so good I don't see why they want to change him.

Mind you, there are a lot of them and they wear big black hats called a *busby*. People come from all over the place to see them, especially when the band plays and they march up and down.

It was so crowded I
had a job to see, so
I tried crawling
between people's
legs and a small
boy mistook me
for a *busby*. Luckily
he didn't try to put me
on his head otherwise
he would have had a shock.

But the best time of all came after the
ceremony was over and most of the crowd had
gone. I was invited into the Palace courtyard
so that Mr Gruber could take my photograph
alongside one of the guards.

He thinks perhaps the Queen likes bears and
she had seen me out of one of the Palace windows

after all, but we shall never know.

Before I went to bed that night I put my Wellington boots on and tried marching up and down my bedroom, but it wasn't the same without a band. Then someone – I think it might have been Mrs Bird – began knocking on the ceiling below me whenever I came to attention, so I had to pretend I was looking for my pyjamas, but it had been a very lovely day.

love from
Paddington

Letter No. 8

Dear Aunt Lucy,

Mr Gruber's shop is usually busiest at the end of the week, except during the summer months when the market is full of tourists, and because most of them are far from home – some from the other side of the world – they aren't interested in buying antiques, so he often closes his shop for the day.

When that happens he likes nothing better than showing me round London, so our next day out was to Hampton Court Palace.

It makes Buckingham Palace seem small.

Everything about it is large, including a king called Henry the Eighth who used to live there. He had a lot of wives, which I expect is why there are so many rooms because he used to get tired of them very quickly.

Mr Gruber showed me a bed where Queen Anne had slept. There was a rope round it which

I thought must have been put there to stop her falling out during the night, but he told me it was to stop visitors getting in. I suppose if you are a queen you have to watch out for that kind of thing.

I think little things like that are very interesting.

From there we saw round the kitchens, where there are huge ovens. Mr Gruber said it must have been where they made Royal buns. Unfortunately they weren't doing it the day we were there, which was a pity. He laughed when I said that if they were to engage a few bears they would have them up and running in no time at all.

Next on the list of things to see was the Royal maze which is entirely made of hedges and is said to be the biggest and oldest in the whole wide world.

I was upset because Mr Gruber had to pay extra before we were allowed in. I think it's wrong to charge for going into a place and then make it as hard as possible to find your way out.

Once again, if they had a bear running it he would let people go in for free and make them buy a ticket in order to get out, charging extra the longer it took them to find the exit.

Mr Gruber looked very impressed when I told him. "I can see I'm in the wrong business, Mr Brown," he said. "We had better do it as quickly as possible," he added, looking at his watch. "Mrs Bird will wonder where we've got to if we take too long."

I didn't want Mr Gruber to get into trouble, so I made sure we didn't get lost.

When we came out the man in the ticket

office said it was the fastest he'd ever seen anyone do it. "You can't have been right to the middle and back," he said.

But we had! I put marmalade chunks on the bushes as we went past them on the way in, and I followed them all the way back on the way out, but don't tell anybody.

Mr Gruber said there are no flies on bears, but I expect there are a lot in the maze by now, especially when it's a hot day!

love from
Paddington

Letter No. 9

Dear Aunt Lucy,

I haven't told you this before, but a few weeks ago I opened a BANK ACCOUNT!

It was Mr Brown's idea and he should know what he is talking about. He said it was asking for trouble keeping all my savings in a suitcase, even if it does have a secret compartment. Word would soon get around. It would be much better to put it into a bank and forget all about it. The best thing of all is that while the money is in the bank it is not only safe but it earns something called 'interest', which means it gets bigger all the time.

He was right about one thing. I soon forgot all about it, which is why I forgot to tell you I'm afraid.

The trouble began last week when I heard the Browns talking about going on a family holiday, and I thought since they have been very kind to me, why don't I take some money out of my bank account and put it towards the cost.

Once I got the idea I couldn't wait to do it, so the next day I had an early morning bath and took myself along to the nearest Floyds Bank.

I was the first one in and the man behind the counter didn't realise I was there until I took my hat off. As I felt for my account book he caught sight of a marmalade sandwich underneath it and I don't think he was very pleased.

"What a way to treat a Floyds bank book!" he said.

Having explained I always keep a sandwich there in case I have an emergency, I asked him how much interest I had in my account and waited while he looked it up on a computer.

"Ten pence," he said.

"Ten pence!" I repeated, giving him a hard stare.

I could hardly believe my ears and having told him I didn't think it sounded very interesting at all, I asked him how much money there was in my account as a whole.

"Five pounds and twenty-five pence," he said. "You can have it back if you like." And he pushed a note and some coins across the counter.

I tell you, Aunt Lucy, it was like a nightmare. If I couldn't believe my ears a moment before, I couldn't believe my eyes now.

Not only did the note have a different number on it and the coins a different date to the ones I gave them when I opened my account, but the note was old and full of creases and the coins were dirty, whereas I had always kept them polished like I do with my Peruvian centavos.

"That isn't the note I gave you," I said. "That one said you promise to pay the bear his money back on demand. It said so in writing."

"Not bear," said the man. "Bear*er*. That's quite a different matter. It means whoever happens to have it on them at the time."

There was only one thing for it. Mr Gruber

always says when you have a problem you should go straight to the top and don't take 'No' for an answer, so I asked to see Mr Floyd, and do you know what the man said?

"I'm sorry, sir. No one of that name works here! As for your note, there's no knowing where it is by now. It may not even exist. They burn old notes, you know."

That did it! I went straight outside to the nearest telephone kiosk and dialled 999.

A very nice girl asked me which service I required: Police, Fire or Ambulance? So I said all three, please, but especially the fire brigade!

If you ask me, banking isn't as easy as it sounds, but to cut a long story short, as Mr Brown might say, you will be glad to know everything was all right in the end. After all the fuss had died down they gave me some new money and a policeman shook my paw.

He said, "It's a pity there aren't more public-spirited bears about like you, sir. If everyone called for help when they saw anything suspicious we would have a lot less work to do in the long run."

I think he might have had trouble with <u>his</u> bank account at some point and I feel much better now.

love from
Paddington

Letter No. 10

Dear Aunt Lucy,

I'm afraid I have to write this letter standing up as it was Judy's end of term Sports Day yesterday and I did a lot of horse riding in one of the events.

When she apologised for throwing me in at the deep end I thought she had put my name down for a swimming race, which was a bit of a surprise because I didn't have my arm bands with me. However, it turned out to be something called a gymkhana.

She thought that because I came from South America I would be good at riding a horse, but

I explained that South America is a big place and she must be thinking of Argentina where the famous Gaucho riders live, and I didn't know one end of a horse from the other.

"Oh, dear," she said. "Don't tell my geography mistress. I've put you down to ride Black Beauty in the first event. It's in aid of our new school swimming pool and practically everyone, parents and all, are sponsoring you. The famous Olympic rider, Gay Cheeseman, has agreed to act as judge and I've told all the other girls so much about you they can't wait to see you come in first."

After all that, I felt I couldn't let her down.

You should have heard the cheer that went up when I climbed onto Black Beauty's saddle, and there was a louder one still when I disappeared over the other side.

But they were nothing compared to the cheering when I reappeared facing the wrong way. I suppose they all thought I was doing it on purpose.

It soon turned to groans when Mr Cheeseman awarded me four hundred and fifty-two faults for allowing Black Beauty to knock down all the fences. Fancy putting them all in our way like that in the first place! You can't blame her.

I don't think it helped when she came back round and trampled over his best bowler hat that had been lying on the ground ready for the presentation of the prizes.

I don't know how he got the name 'Gay'. He was like Mr Curry on a bad day.

Luckily, Mrs Bird had brought along a hamper full of goodies so we could all enjoy a picnic

lunch. There was a huge selection of sandwiches; cucumber, cheese, ham, liver-sausage; along with an endless supply of ingredients to make your own salad for the main course, followed by meringues.

But by then I was in such a daze I had no idea what I was eating and by the time we got to the end even Mrs Bird's meringues, usually so light they practically melted in your mouth, seemed harder than usual and I had to work to get to the end of mine.

Judy had entered me for the last event. It was called 'Chase me Charley', and to tell you the truth I didn't feel like chasing anyone.

However, as things turned out I needn't have worried.

When I climbed back into the saddle I found Black Beauty was a changed animal from the word 'go'. I can't remember what I whispered in her ear, but I closed my eyes and clung on for dear life as she suddenly took off like the wind and literally sailed over anything that came her way. There was simply no stopping her, and in the background it sounded as though the whole school had erupted. Cries of "Good Old Paddington!" rang out from all directions.

It more than made up for my first time out, and I have no idea how long it might have lasted if Mr Cheeseman hadn't come to my rescue by blowing several blasts on his whistle.

"I have never seen anything quite like it

before," he said, as he helped me down, and then he said something that sounded like "Cor blimey!" and dashed off as though he had a train to catch.

After that Diana Ridgeway, the head girl, came up to congratulate me.

She didn't stay more than a moment or two because Miss Grimshaw, the headmistress, wanted to thank me.

"Stout effort!" she cried. "You're a good egg and you have given our new swimming pool an enormous fillip!" She looked as though she would like to have said more, but she asked to be excused and hurried on her way.

I wished I had brought my special stamp with me, because everybody else wanted my autograph, although I must say they all behaved very well and didn't hang around afterwards asking questions.

Meanwhile, Mrs Bird was packing up what was left in the hamper.

"Mercy me!" she cried. "I packed some garlic before we left. Not just a few cloves but the whole bulb, and it isn't there any more. What *can* have happened to it? *And* there is one meringue left over."

The Browns exchanged glances as the penny slowly dropped.

"Black Beauty must have been trying to escape the fumes," said Mrs Brown.

"I must have eaten it by mistake," I said. "I thought it didn't taste as nice as usual."

"Not as nice as usual!" echoed Mr Brown.

"Paddington must have had quite a lot on his mind one way or another," said Mrs Bird gently, as she handed me the last meringue. "We can't

really blame him.
I suggest we have
the car windows
open on the way
home."

I must admit it was
the best idea I'd heard all day.

love from
Paddington

Letter No. 11

Dear Aunt Lucy,

Since I came to live in England I have heard people say lightning doesn't strike the same place twice, and I don't know whether that's true or not. All I do know is it doesn't apply to school Sports Days. I've been to two already this week.

I suppose it isn't surprising. Schools break up for their summer holidays around the same time, and having been to Judy's Sports Day it wouldn't be fair to give Jonathan's a miss. At least his was different. Instead of having a gymkhana to raise money for a swimming pool, they played a game of cricket in aid of a new cricket pavilion.

Captaining a team of old boys, Mr Brown had challenged a team made up of pupils from the sixth form, and the event was being umpired by Alf Duckham, a famous old time cricketer who was known for his fairness.

Listening to all the talk taking place when we arrived it sounded as though Mr Brown's team had a very short old boy and I was beginning to feel worried in case he couldn't see over the stumps, when I realised they were in fact missing one old boy who'd had to drop out at the last moment.

It didn't occur to me that I might be invited to take his place, although I did hear Jonathan's headmaster say, "He's not even an old bear, let alone an old boy."

Which was when I heard Jonathan say, "Please, sir. He likes anything new and he's never played cricket before."

I think Mrs Bird was right when she said he was probably trying to outdo his sister.

Anyway, before I had time to sit down, I found myself standing on what they call the boundary waiting for something to happen. Luckily I had thought to pack a marmalade sandwich under my hat in case I had an emergency, which is how I came to miss my first catch. I think they might have waited!

The ball didn't come my way again before the interval, when the sixth form declared leaving the old boys and myself one hundred and fifty runs to get before the end of the afternoon.

During the first half the sports master had found a pair of old pads he had cut in half so that I could wear them when I went out to bat. It was very kind of him, but it was hard to picture myself doing much running in them because I couldn't bend my legs at the knees. I suppose that's why you don't see many bears playing cricket.

One way and another things were getting gloomier in the old pavilion and I could see why it might be nice to have a bright new one. Even Mrs Bird, who admits she doesn't know anything about cricket, could see that all was not well as one by one old boys came and went.

"Perhaps Paddington will be able to score a run or two," she said, glancing up from her knitting.

"He's last man in," said Jonathan. "And with just over twenty runs to get, I doubt it. 'Smasher' Knowles, the Demon of the Upper Sixth is bowling and he's so fast Paddington won't even see the ball. He's like an express train in his run up. Look … there goes Dad's wicket!"

I made my way out to the crease as fast as I could in the circumstances.

"Best of luck, Paddington," called Mr Brown as we passed. "Don't forget, whatever you do keep a straight bat and keep an eye on the field. Watch where the captain has placed his men. There's a silly mid-off and he has a short leg."

"Say when you're ready," said Alf Duckham when I reached the wicket.

"I'm alright, Mr Duckham," I said. "But I'm a bit worried about the silly mid-off."

Having said that, I must say I didn't like the look on 'Smasher' Knowles' face, so made sure I held my bat straight up in front of myself and closed my eyes. I heard the pounding of feet and seconds later the bat was nearly knocked out of my paws. It was followed by a roar from the crowd.

I opened my eyes and something wonderful had happened. The ball must have gone over the boundary in a direction nobody else had expected.

'Smasher' Knowles was glaring at me. "I can't bowl that bear if he hides behind his pads," he exclaimed crossly. "I can't even see him, let alone the wicket."

Mr Duckham signalled him back to his place. "Everyone has their own way of playing," he said sternly. "This young bear is entitled to his."

It took them a little time to find the ball and the minutes ticked away, but when play began again I went through the same routine. I closed my eyes, there was a pounding of feet, the bat was nearly knocked out of my paws, and a roar went up the crowd.

The ball must have gone in a completely different direction, but once again it was outside the ground and 'Smasher' Knowles was dancing up and down with rage. "Look at him!" he cried. "He's holding his bat the wrong way round. He's got the curved side facing outwards. He doesn't even try to hit the ball. I hit the bat."

"That bear has his methods," said Mr Duckham, signalling another six runs. "I don't know of any rule to say he shouldn't hold it that way."

I expect you are wondering who came out on top. Well, it got so complicated even 'Smasher'

Knowles agreed the only answer was to call it a draw, and Mr Duckham suggested I retire at my peak, then not many other batsmen in the world could say they had a batting average like mine.

Mrs Bird says he is such a nice man and she can see now why he was known for his fairness. I think she might take up cricket!

love from
Paddington

Letter No. 12

Dear Aunt Lucy,

You will never guess what happened last week. To celebrate Jonathan and Judy coming home for the summer holidays Mr Brown took us all to the theatre. As you know, I have never been to a theatre before, and I don't suppose I ever shall again after what happened.

I heard Mr Brown on the telephone booking our seats and he was asking them for a box. I thought how nice  it was of him. I expected it would be for me to stand on so that I didn't miss anything. But it turned out to be a very small room high up in the theatre and I didn't need one anyway.

English is a funny language. They don't waste words – they make them have lots of different meanings instead. But it can be complicated.

They wouldn't let me in at first because I had my suitcase with me. As you know, I'm never without it. I opened it up to show there was nothing to see inside apart from some marmalade sandwiches and I gave them a hard stare so they relented.

It reminded me of the time when I was helping Mr Curry with some plumbing. Having given me a hammer to hold, he pointed towards a join in the piping and said, "When I nod my head, you hit it."

You wouldn't believe the fuss he made when I did what he said!

Anyway, as it was Mr Brown's birthday I thought it would be nice to do something for him so when we were all seated I opened the secret compartment in my suitcase and took out those centavos you gave me in case I had an emergency. I haven't spent any, but I have been keeping them polished.

So when a girl came into our box I seized my chance. She was called an *usherette* and I thought at first it meant she went around telling people to hush if they were making a noise, but it was another of those words I was telling you about and she was selling programmes, so I ordered six – one for each of us.

"That will be twenty-four pounds," she said. "And I don't take foreign coins."

Would you believe it? It's a good job I wasn't standing on a box – I would have fallen off it with the shock.

In the end we settled for one programme we could hand around, which Mr Brown paid for himself, so I was glad I had brought a torch.

As soon as the lights in the theatre went down I switched it on to look for a sandwich. Some people in another box next door to ours began making shushing noises at us as though it was making a noise, so I pointed it in their direction and several people in the back of the theatre began to boo.

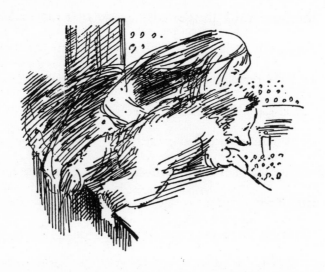

I think the interval, when the lights came back on and I could look down on all the other people, was the best bit.

Judy suggested I might like to try counting them. She promised to give me ten pence if I got up to a hundred before the lights went down again. I managed to get up to twenty-three, but I was so excited I was leaning over the side of the box and I accidentally let go of a marmalade sandwich. It landed on a man's head in the stalls. Luckily he was bald so it didn't make much mess.

"I expect he thinks a bird must have got into the theatre," said Judy.

"I expect it's put him off going to the theatre for the rest of the year," said Jonathan, as we hid ourselves from view.

I don't suppose I shall be going again for a while either.

love from
Paddington

Letter No. 13

Dear Aunt Lucy,

My best friend, Mr Gruber, likes what he calls proverbs. He says they are all tried and tested and if you follow their advice you can't go far wrong in life. So when I arrived at his shop extra early

yesterday morning and he said, "Ah, Mr Brown, *the early bird catches the worm,*" I wasn't at all surprised. I like being early anyway because I buy the buns on my way there and they are still warm.

What did surprise me was he didn't look up when I entered his shop, until I realised he was holding a china dish up to the light and trying to marry it with a small chip that had broken away from the rim.

Having listened to him dealing with customers as much as I have has taught me a lot about antiques, so I knew straight away it was Italian Blue Bone China from the Second Spode Period.

"I'm afraid there's many a slip twixt cup and lip," said Mr Gruber glumly.

"I could try gluing it for you," I said. "Bears are good at gluing things."

"It's very kind of you, Mr Brown," he said. "But I do have some more downstairs. What would really be of help, after we have had our elevenses of course, is if you could take the pieces round to a colleague of mine who specialises in adhesives. Tell him we need something that won't set hard straight away, which will give us a bit of leeway for the time being.

"I would go myself, but I daren't leave the shop. We have an early morning planeload of antique hunters from the other side of the Atlantic paying us a visit. Unfortunately, they all seem to be down at the other end of the market and I need to find some way of attracting them up here."

While he was talking Mr Gruber placed several layers of soft material in my shopping basket on wheels and laid the china gently on top of it.

"I wouldn't trust anyone else with this, Mr Brown," he said, "but I know you won't let me down."

A mug of cocoa and two buns later I was making my way down the Portobello Road when I happened to catch sight of an interesting looking notice in Mr Sloop's barber's shop window.

However, it was a case of 'first things first', so I decided to take a closer look on my way back.

Mr Gruber's friend knew exactly what was needed, and he gave me a large tube of whatever it was, so I was back outside Mr Sloop's sooner than expected, and I saw exactly what Mr Gruber meant when he said that end of the Portobello Road was already crowded. It was like a Saturday afternoon near Christmas.

The notice in his window said WILLING JUNIOR WANTED – URGENTLY, and I had only just finished reading it when the door opened and Mr Sloop himself ushered me inside, shopping basket on wheels and all.

"What can I do for you, sir?" he said. "Short, back and sides, or would you like one of our 'all-in specials'? Haircut, shampoo and set – all for a fiver. You won't know yourself when you look in the mirror."

I pulled my hat down tight in case he began work on my whiskers and announced I had come about the job.

"Blimey!" said Mr Sloop. He looked me up and down. "I suppose I could stand you in the window like one of them 'before and after' advertisements. No prizes for guessing which you'd be."

I gave him one of my hardest ever stares and he immediately changed his tune.

"Hair all over the floor is my big problem," he said. "It needs sweeping up all the time. If I was to give you a broom perhaps you could have a go while I pop out and get a morning coffee." He gave me a funny look. "Some people might think it's a lot of work for five pounds a week."

"Five pounds!" I repeated, hardly able to believe my ears. "*Every* week? That's over forty buns."

"Done, then," said Mr Sloop. "Mind you, it's only a trial. But if it works out I might let you have a go with the clippers in a day or two. Meanwhile, the broom is in the cupboard so you can start by making yourself useful."

And with that he left me on my own.

Apart from the broom, there were rows and rows of bottles and jars, and by the time I had unscrewed the caps on several of them to see what was inside it was a while before I came out.

Much to my surprise a man was already sitting in the barber's chair.

"I'd like a trim please," he said. "Not too little and not too much. Don't touch the top and make it snappy. I've been up all night."

He gave a loud yawn followed by a gentle snore.

I must say, Aunt Lucy, Mr Brown often goes to sleep very quickly after one of Mrs Bird's Sunday lunches, but never as fast as that. So, having unloaded Mr Gruber's china onto a shelf for safe keeping, I was looking for some scissors when I came across an electric razor, plugged in and ready to go.

I knew it was ready to go because when I picked it up it made a purring noise. Better still, when I put it against the back of the man's neck a lovely white path appeared, which was very interesting.

Mr Sloop had told me to make myself useful, so I took a quick look over my shoulder to see if he was anywhere around and by the time I looked back something dreadful had happened.

The man had told me not to touch the top of his head, but it was too late. Whereas it had been covered by a mass of thick black curls, now there wasn't a hair to be seen. He was completely bald!

There was only one thing for it. I reached for my tube. Mr Sloop had said his floor was covered with unwanted hair, so I wouldn't be short of material to repair the damage.

It seemed like a good idea at the time, but there were so many different kinds of hair, and so many different colours it didn't go as well as I had hoped. Even so, I wasn't prepared for the bellow of rage that came from the man when he woke up and saw his reflection in the mirror. His eyes

nearly popped out of his head and he jumped out of the chair and made a dive for the nearest object to hand as though he intended to throw it across the room.

"Watch out!" I cried. "That's Mr Gruber's Spode."

He froze. "Did I hear you say it's a Spode?"

"From their Blue Italian Bone China Range," I said. "Circa 1860."

"And you know this Gruber?"

"He's my best friend," I said. "He's an antique dealer."

"Take me to him," said the man. "That's the kind of thing I'm over here for, with all the other guys, but I wouldn't mind getting there first. They can follow on after."

I did as I was bidden, and having seen

Mr Gruber's things safely back to the shop, along with Mr Sloop's customer, I made myself scarce before his friends arrived.

I didn't see him to talk to again that day, but I went as early as possible the following day.

"Just in time to solve a mystery," he said. "Not much happens in the market that we don't hear about and it seems Mr Sloop was sweeping out his shop this morning when he came across a big black hairpiece. I gather you were in there yesterday and I wondered if you had any ideas."

"A hairpiece?" I repeated.

"It's another name for a wig," said Mr Gruber. "Some men don't like it when they go bald, so they cover it up. He can't think where it came from."

"Oh, dear…" I began.

Mr Gruber held up his hand. "Say no more,

Mr Brown. I can't thank you enough for what you did yesterday. I haven't been so busy for a long time and lots of happy customers went on their way. Mine is not to reason how it all came about.

"There's another old saying that could be said to fit the bill on this occasion: *Least said – soonest mended.*" And with that he put a finger to his lips and we settled down to our cocoa and buns.

love from
Paddington

Letter No. 14

Dear Aunt Lucy,

Apart from Mrs Bird's home-made marmalade, one of the nicest things about living with the Browns is that no two days are ever the same. That's not to say there aren't days when the same thing happens more than once. On days like that you don't know whether you are coming or going; like today for example.

It all began when I found the letter-box in the front door half open because someone had tried to push a magazine through and it was stuck, so I tried removing it, and while I had my paw under the flap I peered through the gap to see if the postman was anywhere in sight.

I didn't want a repeat of what happened the other day when someone – I think it may have been Mr Gruber – sent me an Advent calendar (it certainly wouldn't have been Mr Curry) and half the doors on it were wide open.

Anyway, the postman was nowhere in sight, but I was just in time to catch a glimpse of the longest car I have ever seen in my life going past. It was black all over, including the windows, which meant that although it was going very slowly, as though the person or persons inside were looking for somebody, I couldn't see a soul.

In fact, the car was so long I thought it would never end, and because Jonathan and Judy were home for the Christmas holidays, I rushed to tell them.

Judy said it sounded like a limousine, so it must be someone important, and Jonathan said he didn't like the sound of it on account of 'my circs'.

When I asked what 'my circs' were he said, "Well, the fact is, Paddington, you were a stowaway, so you won't have the right papers. We're worried stiff that one day they might come and take you away. If it happens again hide behind the curtains and leave us to do the talking."

Half an hour later I looked through the letter-box just in case and there it was again, only this time it had stopped outside our house, so I did as Jonathan said and dropped everything.

I was only just in time, for there was a ring at the bell followed by the sound of voices, and for a while it seemed as though everyone in the house was talking at once. I hardly dared draw breath until at long last Judy found where I was hiding and I was able to fill up my lungs.

"You're not going to believe this," she said. "But it's your Uncle Pastuzo. He's going round the world, so he thought he would call in and say hullo."

"Uncle Pastuzo!" I said. "Come to see me?" For a moment or two I could hardly believe my ears.

"The trouble is," said Jonathan, "he likes doing things in style so he hired that enormously long car yesterday. You want to look inside. It's full of gadgets – like something out of James Bond. He's been driving round and round ever since because he couldn't find any gaps large enough to park near us. *And*, he says, we have rules in this country about which side of the road we drive on, which makes it very confusing.

"Then he saw Mr Curry going out, so he's parked across his driveway too."

But my mind was still in such a whirl all I could say was, "I hope he hasn't overlapped too much.

You know what Mr Curry's like. He'll blame me."

"I shouldn't worry on that score," said Judy. "Your uncle won't stand for any nonsense. Apparently he made his fortune high up in the Peruvian Andes looking after miners digging for gold and other precious metals. They are a tough lot, but when they come up for air at the end of their shift they pay anything for an ice-cold mineral, so he has built up a thriving business."

"Perhaps he'll give Mr Curry a bottle of lemonade," said Jonathan.

"I can't wait to see him," I said. "What's he like?"

"Well," said Judy. "He's a funny mixture. When he arrived he threw his hat across the room and as it landed on top of a standard lamp he said, 'Home is where you hang your hat.' Which made us think he was staying a long time.

"Then, when Mum wanted to show him to his room, he said he didn't mean to be a nuisance so could he sleep in the summer house?"

"He wouldn't hear of anything else," said Jonathan. "He has his own folding bed, so Dad's helping to remove the lawn mower while Mrs Bird gets his breakfast. Listen to what happened next..."

"Mercy me, *Signor* Pastuzo!" said Judy, imitating Mrs Bird's voice when she heard he hadn't had anything to eat that morning. "You can have anything you like. Bacon and eggs ... kippers ... sausages ... kedgeree ... fried potato ... black pudding ... toast and marmalade ..."

"Guess what he said?" broke in Jonathan. "Sounds great to me, *señorita*!"

"Mrs Bird went quite pink when he kissed her hand," said Judy. "She said, 'Good manners run in the family,' and disappeared into the kitchen. We haven't seen her since."

Now, here's where the great mystery begins, Aunt Lucy. I was talking to Uncle Pastuzo this evening and I asked him about my 'circs' and what important documents I need and where they might be, so he said, "leave it with me, *sobrino*," and went out to his car.

When he came back he told me you had said all I had to do was look in the secret compartment of my suitcase. Everything I need is in there.

Now, what I don't know is how Uncle Pastuzo was able to speak to you when there isn't a telephone in the Home for Retired Bears.

I asked Jonathan and he said there is a computer

in the car and that perhaps he knows someone connected with the Home who has one and they sent each other messages.

I couldn't picture a car having a computer, but Jonathan said it isn't a big one like Mr Brown's. It's what is called a 'lap-top'.

I said it can't belong to one of the bears then, because bears don't have laps, they have knees.

"In that case," he said, "it might be someone with a knee-top computer – we shall probably never know."

Anyway, I looked in my secret compartment and there they all were: passport and everything!

The best thing about it was the look on Mrs Bird's face when she set eyes on them. She said she always knew you wouldn't let me down over such an important matter, Aunt Lucy, and

to thank you very much. That night we had a party to celebrate the occasion so I didn't go to bed until after nine o'clock.

love from
Paddington

P. S. Uncle Pastuzo says he is planning an outing for all of us tomorrow. I will tell you about it in my next letter.

Letter No. 15

Dear Aunt Lucy,

Uncle Pastuzo's outing must have taken longer to organise than he expected because he was out all the morning and he didn't reappear until the middle of the afternoon, when it was already beginning to get dark.

If you ask me, that made it all the more exciting because, as Jonathan said, we were all on tenderhooks by then, although Mr Brown, who doesn't like to be kept waiting, pointed out that the word is tenterhooks, which is a device manufacturers use to stretch cloth whereas, big though the car was, now there were eight of us in the party, each with a window seat, there wasn't that much room for stretching.

The extra numbers came about because Uncle Pastuzo had engaged a chauffeur, and he had very kindly invited Mr Gruber along too. I think he was hoping he might provide a running commentary.

Mrs Bird took against the curtains, which she said didn't match the carpet and anyway they were far too grand, while Mrs Brown wanted them drawn for fear of what the neighbours might think if they saw us setting off in such style.

But finally we all settled down and were on our way.

I asked Mr Gruber if he knew where we were going, but he wasn't letting on. "It is something

I have always wanted to do, Mr Brown," was all he would say.

By then we had come to a complete stop on a pedestrian crossing in Notting Hill Gate and with a sea of faces pressed against the windows on both sides everybody went quiet.

Uncle Pastuzo looked at his watch. "We are due for take-off in thirty minutes," he said to the chauffeur. Which had us all thinking we were heading for an airport and we were going to be late. We couldn't have been more wrong.

However, by general consent he pressed a button and all the curtains slid together. They stayed that way, shutting us off from the outside world for the next twenty minutes or so when we eventually came to a halt and the chauffeur switched the engine off.

"It is the only way in this kind of car," said Uncle Pastuzo.

Jonathan and Judy gave a gasp as they looked out, but as I joined them expecting to see rows of aeroplanes, all I could make out was what looked like a giant bicycle wheel in the sky.

"It's the London Eye," said Judy excitedly.

"We are all going for a ride on it," explained Mr Gruber.

Mrs Brown looked as though she wished she'd brought her smelling salts, and I must say I was worried we might get a puncture.

"No fear of either," said Jonathan. "It hasn't fallen over yet, and there's nothing to get a puncture."

"Those pods with people inside them may look as though they are made of glass," said Judy. "But they aren't of course, and it does mean you can see everything as you go round."

"There are thirty-two of them," said Uncle Pastuzo, reading from a sheet of paper. "Each pod holds up to twenty-five passengers, and you know what? I have booked one all to ourselves.

"I fix everything," he continued, as a hostess came forward to greet us. "We take what is called the VIP trip. Tee hee!"

"Tee hee?" repeated Mrs Brown.

"Ought to be VIB – Very Important Bears!"

Doubled up with laughter at his own joke, Uncle Pastuzo saw us all safely on the first empty pod when it arrived, and as the doors closed behind us we moved ever so slowly on our way.

The sun disappeared behind the Houses of Parliament and Mr Gruber came into his own, pointing out the important landmarks not just to Uncle Pastuzo, but to all of us; Buckingham Palace and other places we had been to on our outings; Big Ben; St Paul's Cathedral and the many parks and green spaces that were not generally to be seen at ground level.

As we rose higher and higher and lights began to appear all over London the streets looked as though they were peopled by ants and the

buildings became tiny models of the real thing.
Christmas lights twinkled in the night sky.

They were never to be repeated magical
moments and we all agreed Uncle Pastuzo's

timing couldn't have been better. As the hostess began handing out refreshments, Mr Brown made a little speech apologising if we had been a trifle impatient earlier and thanking Uncle Pastuzo for providing us with such a wonderful experience. We are very lucky people.

Uncle Pastuzo beamed with pleasure, "*Amigos,*" he said. "It is the only way to see the world. From on high and away from the crowds. Have another chocolate éclair."

It was during the journey home that he broke the news he would be moving on the next day and everyone in the car became downcast.

It took me a while before I realised why they were quite so gloomy. It was something I overheard Judy say. They wondered if I might be leaving with him, and that decided me.

When we got back to Windsor Gardens I hurried upstairs and put a large nail in the back of my bedroom door. It was a souvenir of my decorating and I knew it might come in useful one day.

I went to bed extra early that night and when everyone else crept in one by one to say 'goodnight' I waited until they were all there before I removed my hat.

"Don't worry," I said, as I threw it towards the nail as Uncle Pastuzo might have done. "Home is where you hang your hat."

Unfortunately it landed on my own head and everybody laughed.

"Never mind, Paddington," said Mrs Bird, amid general agreement and sighs of relief all round. "As your good friend, Mr Gruber, would have it, 'There is a lot of truth in the old sayings and never more so than *It's the thought that counts*'."

love from
Paddington

HOME FOR RETIRED BEARS, LIMA

Dear Readers,

Having reached the end of this book, it struck me that some of you must be wondering why, when I sent Paddington off on a voyage of discovery (and I can't tell you what a wrench that was), I chose to put him on a boat bound for England, hoping he might end up in London.

Well! Thereby hangs a tale as the saying goes.

In the highlands of Peru, some 12,500 feet above sea level, there is a huge lake called Lake Titicaca. It is the largest stretch of inland water in the whole of South America. So large in fact, the 'powers that be' decided they needed a boat to get from one end of it to the other, so they ordered one to be built for them in England.

I don't think they had really thought the whole thing through, though, because it turned out to be so big – over 200 tonnes – the makers couldn't send it all at once. It began to arrive in bits and pieces with instructions for putting it together on Lake Titicaca itself. Worse still, the last 350 kilometres of the journey was by means of mules. They could only cope with a small amount at a time, so the whole thing took place over a number of years rather than

months. You can picture what an upheaval that meant to the countryside while it was happening.

All that took place some one hundred and fifty years or so ago, but while the work was going on a wealthy English explorer happened to be in the area and he was so upset at the way bears were being uprooted from their normal habitat he set up a fund for them. At the same time he bought a huge empty house on Lima's sea front to take care of the older ones who had nowhere to go. So you will understand why we have a soft spot for anything British. Nobody ever treated us like that before.

We have a small lending library in our Rest Room at the Home for Retired Bears. (When I say *small*, at the last count there were only five books.) They are really meant for the oldest inhabitants when they are at a loose end. But since most of them can't read, they make use of them for 'other purposes' – like doorstops when there is a gale blowing.

Anyway, among the books still available there is one with a list of famous sayings, and in it there is one by a Mr Boswell, who said, "When a man is tired of London, he is tired of life; for there is in London all that life can afford."

I thought he must know what he is talking about, and if London is good enough for him it probably applies to bears as well. It seems to be working out very well, so I have written to him to say 'thank you', but I am still waiting for a reply.

Yours truly,

Aunt Lucy

Michael Bond

A Bear Called
Paddington

Illustrated by Peggy Fortnum

The first adventures of Paddington Bear

Paddington Bear had travelled all the way from
Darkest Peru when the Brown family first met
him on Paddington station. Since then their
lives have never been quite the same…

Michael Bond

More About
Paddington

Illustrated by Peggy Fortnum

The original adventures of Paddington Bear

When Paddington attempts home decorating,
detective work and photography, the Brown
family soon find that he causes his own
particular brand of chaos.

Michael Bond

Paddington
Helps Out

Illustrated by Peggy Fortnum

The original adventures of Paddington Bear

"*Oh, dear!*" said Paddington,
"*I'm in trouble again.*"

Trouble always comes naturally to Paddington.
What other bear could catch a fish in his hat,
or cause havoc in the Browns' kitchen
just trying to be helpful?

Michael Bond

Paddington
Abroad

Illustrated by Peggy Fortnum

The original adventures of Paddington Bear

The Browns are going abroad and a certain bear
is planning the trip. But, as Mrs Brown worries,
with Paddington in charge, "*There's no knowing
where we might end up!*"

Michael Bond

Paddington
at Large

Illustrated by Peggy Fortnum

The original adventures of Paddington Bear

"*Even Paddington can't come to much harm in
half an hour,*" said Mrs Brown.

But who else could hang Mr Curry's
lawnmower from a treetop or set Father
Christmas' beard on fire?

Michael Bond

Paddington
Here and Now

Illustrated by Peggy Fortnum and R.W. Alley
The original adventures of Paddington Bear

"*I'm not a foreigner,*" exclaimed Paddington,
"*I'm from Darkest Peru.*"

One day, a mysterious visitor arrives at number
thirty-two Windsor Gardens. Is it time for
Paddington to decide where 'home' really is?

Michael Bond

Paddington
Races Ahead

Illustrated by Peggy Fortnum *and* R.W. Alley

The original adventures of Paddington Bear

Find out what happens when Paddington
causes a London bus to be evacuated,
and is mistaken for a Peruvian hurdler!